Horror Holiday

With special thanks to Jim Collins

First published in Great Britain in 2013 by Buster Books,
an imprint of Michael O'Mara Books Limited,
9 Lion Yard, Tremadoc Road, London SW4 7NQ

www.busterbooks.co.uk
www.monstrousmaud.co.uk

Series created by Working Partners Limited
Text copyright © Working Partners Limited 2013

Cover design by Nicola Theobald

Illustration copyright © Buster Books 2013
Illustrations by Sarah Horne

HOUSE OF DEATH™ copyright © House Industries

A CIP catalogue record for this book is available
from the British Library.

ISBN: 978–1–78055–172–2

1 3 5 7 9 10 8 6 4 2

Papers used by Michael O'Mara Books are natural,
recyclable products made from wood grown in sustainable forests.
The manufacturing processes conform to the environmental
regulations of the country of origin.

Printed and bound in January 2013 by CPI Group (UK) Ltd,
108 Beddington Lane, Croydon, CR0 4YY, United Kingdom

Horror Holiday

A. B. Saddlewick

BUSTER

Chapter One

Bump! The car bounced and clanked along. "Ow! Slow down, Daddy!" grumbled Milly Montague. "That's the third time I've banged my head!"

Maud wished her sister would stop making a fuss. She travelled down this road in the school bus almost every day, and that was a hundred times bumpier.

"Sorry," said Mr Montague. "I thought the suspension could handle it, but this road isn't up to much. Look at the size of those potholes! The council should do something about it."

Maud smiled as she remembered the day a group of workers had been sent to fix the road. They'd hardly got their tools out before Mr Quasimodo, the school caretaker, tried to offer them a cup of tea. They'd run away screaming.

Maud looked down at her blazer pocket, where her pet rat Quentin was bobbing up and down like a baby kangaroo. He peered up at her and squeaked with fear.

"Don't worry, Quent," she said. "It'll be over soon."

Not soon enough, though. Maud had been dreading tonight for weeks. She'd tried to stop her mum and dad from coming to parents' evening, but they'd insisted. They were bound to find out that Rotwood was a monster school! And if they did, they'd forbid her from ever going back.

The aroma of rotting leaves and stagnant puddles drifted into the car.

"Put the windows up!" shouted Milly, lifting

her pink blouse up over her nose. "Maud's school is already making me sick. I don't know why you had to bring me."

"Sorry, petal," said Mrs Montague, "but we've found it very difficult to get babysitters since the incident with Tracy."

"The poor girl is still convinced she was attacked by a flying hamster with fangs," said Mr Montague. "All her friends think our house is haunted now. Won't even come for double pay!"

Maud felt a little guilty that Tracy had been so scared of the vampire hamster she'd been looking after. But she couldn't tell her parents what had really happened that evening. Not without revealing the truth about Rotwood.

"I just don't understand why I'm being punished," said Milly. "Shouldn't I be rewarded for getting straight As in my report?"

"This isn't a punishment, dear. What about our holiday?" asked Mrs Montague. "Doesn't that count as a reward?"

"I suppose so," said Milly. "Though it will have to be pretty flipping amazing to make up for this pong."

"Watch your language, young lady," said Mr Montague. "We don't use words like 'flipping' in this family."

"Very flipping sorry," muttered Milly under her breath.

"And it just so happens that I have some good news on the holiday front," Mr Montague went on. "You know how I said we might be going to Corfu?"

Maud pricked up her ears.

"Yes?" asked Milly, leaning forward.

"Well, all the flights were fully booked," said Mr Montague. "So we're going to the Classic Car Show instead. Isn't that fantastic?"

Maud's heart sank, and for once, her sister was speechless.

"No need to thank me," said Mr Montague. "It'll be fun for everyone! After all, who'd want to lounge around on a beach when they could be learning about the history of motoring? And it was cheaper, too, if you can believe it."

Milly rolled her eyes and slumped in her seat.

The car's headlights picked out a sign ahead:

ROTWOOD SCHOOL
BECAUSE WE SCARE

"Some practical joker has added an 's' in front of 'care'," said Mr Montague, chuckling to himself.

"Er … yes," said Maud. "Great joke, isn't it?"

The thick trees on either side fell away and the bumpy road turned to gravel.

Rotwood loomed ahead of them. The sky was growing dark, and Maud thought the building's spiky stone towers and arched windows looked more bleak and forbidding than ever.

"What a disgusting dump," said Milly. "It's even more rubbish than I was expecting."

"Well, I think it looks very cosy," said Mrs Montague cheerfully. "Though a few lights wouldn't go amiss."

Maud winced as she looked at the weird array of vehicles parked outside. There was a horse and carriage that looked as if it had ridden in from Victorian days; a row of rusty penny-farthing bikes with huge wheels at the front and tiny ones at the back; and a couple of broomsticks perched against the wall.

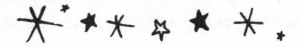

As Mr Montague parked, Maud noticed that a hearse with a wooden coffin in the back had just arrived. Her half-vampire friend Paprika got out, straightened his cape and opened the back door. The coffin creaked open and his mum rose from it, shaking the soil from her ballgown.

"Our playing fields are over there," said Maud quickly, pointing in the opposite direction.

"That's where we play totally normal games like netball and tennis."

Mrs Montague squinted into the darkness. "I can't really see anything, petal. But I'm sure they're very nice."

Maud glanced over her shoulder and saw that Paprika and his mum had gone into the school. She sighed. They hadn't even gone inside yet, and already it was proving difficult to keep the truth about Rotwood hidden.

They all got out of the car and crunched across the gravel. As Maud glanced up at the hulking grey school, one of the stone gargoyles winked at her.

It was going to be a long night.

Chapter Two

Mr Montague headed towards the front steps. "Look at this monster!" he said.

Maud stopped dead in her tracks. She couldn't believe her dad had discovered the truth already.

"I bet it didn't have any trouble at all on that dreadful road," continued Mr Montague.

Maud turned and saw that her dad was admiring a huge red truck with massive wheels and a gleaming chrome grille.

Maud wondered whose truck it was. It seemed way too cool to belong to any of the teachers.

"Come along, dear," said Mrs Montague. "You'll have plenty of time for all that at the Car Show."

Milly scowled.

Maud climbed the large steps into the gloomy entrance hall. Hundreds of pupils and parents were milling around in the flickering light of the wall-mounted torches.

Mrs Montague paused to look at a display of paintings by some of the school's youngest monsters. There was a giant spider with a row of yellow eyes, a three-headed dog, and a lion with wings.

"These are very vivid," said Mrs Montague. "Was the theme 'nightmares'?"

"Yep, got it in one," said Maud. The theme had actually been 'favourite pets'.

The caretaker, Mr Quasimodo, stomped towards them with a clipboard. He had made an effort to dress up for parents' evening, but Maud didn't think it was quite working. His black trousers stopped just above his ankles and his jacket was stretched so tight over the hunch on his back that it was splitting at the seams. He was wearing a clean white shirt, but it only made his skin look greener.

"Wh … what's that?" asked Milly.

"Ssh! It's who, not what," whispered Maud. "Mr Quasimodo is the school caretaker."

Paprika's mum stepped over to the caretaker, jabbing her finger into his chest and scolding him about the state of the poison ivy garden.

"I know he looks a bit strange," said Maud. "But he's alright really."

"Yeah, he's harmless," said Paprika, who had appeared behind them. "He hasn't eaten anyone in years."

Maud stamped hard on Paprika's foot. "No monster stuff," she whispered.

"Oops," muttered Paprika. "Sorry." They took a few steps away, leaving Milly to gape at the terrifying caretaker.

"I don't know if I can keep this up," said Maud, once they were out of earshot. "I just want to have my appointment and go."

"I know how you feel," said Paprika. "Mum goes spare if I get a bad report. Once I got such a bad mark in history that Mum made me fly to school with one wing tied behind my back."

Maud glanced over at Paprika's mother. She was waiting impatiently for Mr Quasimodo to find their appointment on his clipboard. Finally, she snatched it off him and scanned through it herself.

Paprika sighed. "She said that if I don't do well this year, she'll take me out of Rotwood and send me to a boarding school in Transylvania."

"She wouldn't!" said Maud.

Mrs Von Bat swept past and seized Paprika by the arm.

"Gotta go!" he said miserably.

Mr Quasimodo shuffled over. "Names," he grunted.

"Mr and Mrs Maurice Montague," said Maud's dad, holding his hand out.

Mr Quasimodo stared at Mr Montague's hand and licked his lips. His stomach let out a loud rumble.

Mr Montague pulled his hand sharply back.

"Room 3B," said Mr Quasimodo. "At top of staircase. Hurry."

"Thank you, my good man," said Mr Montague.

They all turned towards the spiral staircase, but before they could go, Mr Quasimodo plonked his fat green fingers on Milly's shoulder.

Milly shrieked and squirmed out of his grip.

"My wife has set up crèche in dungeon," he said. "You go there. Have fun."

"D-dungeon?" Milly stammered. "You can't send me to the dungeon. I've done nothing wrong!"

"Oh, it's not a real dungeon!" said Maud. "Don't be silly. That's just a name we give our games room as a joke. You'll love it!"

"That does sound like a good idea," said Mr Montague. "Why would you want to listen to Maud's report anyway?"

"So I can laugh at the bad bits," said Milly. "Obviously."

Mr Quasimodo escorted Milly to the steps leading down to the dungeon. She turned back to look at them, her face turning as green as his. *She'll be fine,* thought Maud. *There's nothing dangerous down there. Well, there is, but hopefully it'll be asleep.*

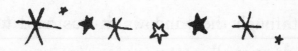

Maud led her parents up the staircase to her classroom. Flaming torches cast long shadows along the curved walls. They passed an arched window overlooking the playground, which was a mess of crumbling headstones.

"Is that a graveyard down there?" asked Mrs Montague.

"Ha ha! Of course not," said Maud, thinking fast. "That's just ... where they store the spare flagstones for the entrance hall."

As they made their way up, Quentin popped his head out of Maud's blazer pocket and squeaked.

"I know how you feel," whispered Maud. "This could be awful."

They reached the top of the stairs, and Maud led her parents along the stone corridor. This place was murky enough in the daytime, but with just the inky evening light seeping in through the windows, it was hard to see anything at all.

"Are you sure this is the right way?" asked Mrs Montague. "Has there been a power cut or something?"

"Mr Quasimodo believes in saving electricity,"

said Maud. "For the sake of the planet."

"Oh," said Mrs Montague. "That's very green of him."

And that's not all that's green about him, thought Maud. They reached the door to Class 3B, and Maud took a deep breath. All it would take was for Mr Von Bat to let the truth slip, and her Rotwood days would be over. No more Fright lessons, no more Monsterball and no more hanging out with Wilf and Paprika.

She lifted a hand and knocked on the door.

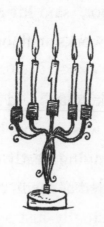

Chapter Three

Maud was just reaching for the handle, when the door creaked open of its own accord.

"Automatic door," said Mr Montague. "Very snazzy. Probably works on floor sensors, doesn't it?"

"Something like that," said Maud.

Mr Von Bat was sitting behind his desk with his cape hanging neatly over the back of his chair. He smiled at them, exposing his fake fangs. He was actually just a normal human, but everyone in Rotwood believed he was a vampire. Maud had hoped he was going to give the bloodsucker stuff a rest tonight, but obviously he hadn't. *I'm doomed*, she thought.

But instead of running away screaming, Mrs Montague ran forward to embrace Mr Von Bat, who blushed and stood up stiffly.

"Norman?" she said. "I had no idea you taught Maud!"

"I'm surprised she never mentioned it," said Mr Von Bat. He quickly spat his plastic fangs into his hand and placed them inside his pocket.

"This is Norman Bottom," said Mrs Montague, turning to Maud's dad. "The nice man who played Dracula in our theatre production last spring. You must remember him."

"Norman Bottom, as I live and breathe!" said Mr Montague. "But why the devil are you still wearing your costume?"

"Because Rotwood is a school for mon …" Mr Von Bat stopped as he spotted Maud shaking her head and gesturing wildly.

"It's because he … er … likes to stay in character," said Maud.

"You stay in character six months after finishing a production?" asked Mr Montague.

"Just to be on the safe side," said Mr Von Bat.

Thank goodness he's going along with it, Maud thought.

"Well, that's commitment for you," said Mr Montague, impressed. "And from what I hear, you're just as committed to teaching our little monster."

"Monster?" asked Mr Von Bat, looking confused. "But Maud isn't a monster. She's just a normal human girl."

"That's very kind of you to say," said Mrs Montague. "Maud seems to be really enjoying herself at Rotwood. You like it here, don't you, cupcake?"

"Yes, I do," said Maud. "I really, really do."

Mr Von Bat sat back down behind his desk and pressed the tips of his fingers together.

Maud and her parents each sat at a desk. "Well," said the teacher, "Maud has been getting on well enough. And I suppose she does have a certain talent when it comes to Fright classes."

"Fright classes?" asked Mrs Montague. "What are they?"

"Art classes!" said Maud, shooting up from her seat. "He meant I'm *fright*fully good at Art."

"Really?" asked Mr Montague, chuckling. "You must have improved since you drew that portrait of me. I thought it was meant to be some sort of demented scarecrow until I saw the word 'Dad' written underneath."

"And she did very well on the last spell test," said Mr Von Bat.

"Spelling test," corrected Maud.

"And she's made good progress in History," said Mr Von Bat. "She wrote a very pleasing essay on the history of vampires."

"The history of what?" asked Mr Montague.

"Umpires," said Maud. "I wrote about the

history of cricket umpires. Fascinating subject."

Wow, thought Maud, *I'm actually getting good at this.*

"Oh," said Mrs Montague. "That all sounds very … er … original."

"Yes indeed, umpires," said Mr Von Bat, wiping his brow. "So all in all Maud's progress has been good. The only slight problem is that she started somewhat late in the school year, so she hasn't gathered enough credits to pass."

Maud sat forward in her chair. This was the first she'd heard about credits.

"And what happens if she doesn't?" asked Mrs Montague.

"Well, unfortunately, she'll have to repeat the year," said Mr Von Bat.

Maud gasped. Repeat the year? They couldn't do that, could they? She'd be separated from Wilf, Paprika and all her other friends …

"Surely you could make an exception?" asked Mrs Montague.

"I'm sorry, but I can't break the rules," said Mr Von Bat. "Even for my amateur dramatics friends."

"I could take extra Fright … I mean Art lessons," said Maud. "Then I'd have enough credits, wouldn't I?"

"I'm afraid not," said Mr Von Bat. "The only way you can pass is if you get ten out of ten on your holiday essay. The topic is 'The Fright of my Life'."

Maud felt like crying. It was almost impossible to get a perfect score. The highest mark she'd got before was a nine.

"Well, thanks for all your help," said Mr Montague, getting to his feet. "I suppose it wouldn't be the end of the world if Maud had to repeat a year."

"And do let us know when your next Dracula performance is," said Mrs Montague.

Maud wanted to say that Mr Von Bat had a Dracula performance every day, but she didn't want to risk annoying him. He had done her a big favour tonight, and she'd have to keep him sweet if she wanted to get full marks.

Maud led her parents out of the room and down the staircase.

"Well, that wasn't too bad, was it, dear?" asked Mrs Montague.

"I suppose not," said Maud. But her mind was already racing about the essay. What could she write that would impress Mr Von Bat enough to give her a ten?

A cold wind was blowing in through the open windows, and some of the torches had gone out, leaving parts of the stairwell in pitch darkness. Maud took her mum's hand and guided her slowly down, sticking closely to the wall, where the steps were widest.

The school nurse, Mrs Quasimodo, was

waiting for them at the bottom. She was wearing a clean white uniform over her scaly green skin. Maud wondered if she'd washed the bloodstains out especially for parents' evening.

Milly was standing next to the nurse, staring straight ahead and trembling. "Jars of eyeballs …" she muttered. "Pickled hands … slimy leeches …"

"What's the matter, cupcake?" asked Mrs Montague, bending down to look Milly in the eye. "What happened to you?"

"She want to play doctors and nurses," growled Mrs Quasimodo. "So I show her school surgery."

"Vats of blood … buckets of fingers … flasks of noses …" continued Milly.

"I think you must have taken my sister to the Art room," said Maud, pulling her family towards the door. "It sounds like she's seen more of the nightmare paintings from last week."

Maud dragged Milly out of the school

doorway, and her parents followed. *Free at last!* Maud thought, as they were walking back towards the car. She made out the figures of a tall man and woman leaning against the red truck with the oversized wheels. They were wearing baseball caps, jeans, leather jackets and dark glasses. The man looked like he was over two metres tall and had a neat brown beard. The woman took off her dark glasses, and Maud noticed she had bushy eyebrows that met in the middle.

Suddenly a dog jumped out of the back seat of the truck on its hind legs. No, wait … It wasn't a dog – it was Maud's werewolf friend, Wilf Wild.

Of course, thought Maud. *No wonder those people are so hairy! They're Wilf's parents.*

"Hi, Maud," said Wilf. "Hi, Mr and Mrs Montague. Nice to meet you."

Maud wondered if her parents would notice that there was something strange about him, but she doubted it. Wilf had thick hair on his face and hands, but he could still pass for an unusual boy. At least they hadn't seen him when there was a full moon, when he'd be running around on all fours and howling.

"How did your report go?" asked Wilf.

"Not great," said Maud. "Mr Von Bat says I need to get ten out of ten on my holiday essay or I'll have to repeat the year."

"Ten out of ten?" asked Wilf. "I've never heard of anyone getting full marks."

Maud's eyes widened. "Never?"

"Nope, it's impossible," said Wilf. His eyes widened and he clapped his hands over his mouth. "Wait, I mean ... sorry. If anyone can do it, it's you."

Next to them, Milly was still mumbling away to herself. "Beakers of ears ... metal drills ... horrible shrieks ..."

"Is she alright?" asked Wilf.

"She's fine," said Maud. "She just banged her head. Anyway, how was your report?"

"Mr Von Bat said I was a good all-rounder, but need to work on my Fright skills," said Wilf. "He said I should try and be as fierce as Warren." He scowled. "I hate it when people say that."

Maud hoped Wilf didn't become more like his brother. Warren was a mean bully who went around growling at anyone who got in his way.

Over by the truck, Maud's parents were chatting to Mr and Mrs Wild.

"This thing must have a beast of an engine inside it," Mr Montague said, patting the front of the truck.

"1500 horsepower," said Mr Wild. "That's 1500 times as much as that horse-drawn carriage over there."

"Wow!" said Mr Montague.

On the other side of the truck, Maud's mum was talking to Mrs Wild about her amateur dramatics society. "We're doing *Les Misérables* next, so as you can imagine, I'm spending a lot of time making wigs."

"If you need any spare hair, let me know," said Mrs Wild. "We've still got a big bag left over from our last shearing."

"Shearing?" asked Mrs Montague. "So you keep sheep, do you?"

"Oh no," said Mrs Wild. "I try to avoid having snacks around. Too much temptation."

Mrs Montague smiled, but she looked a little confused.

Finally snapping out of her daze, Milly scuttled over to Mr Montague and tugged at his sleeve. "I want to go now. I've had enough."

"Looks like the little one is tired," said Mr Montague to the Wilds. "But thanks for your offer. We're looking to go away for the week, so it sounds ideal."

Uh-oh, thought Maud. "What sounds ideal?" she asked.

"Now, I know you were looking forward to the Classic Car Show," said Mr Montague. "But Mr Wild has asked us to go camping in Oddington Marshes with them next week, and I think it's a great idea! It will be a lot cheaper than forking out for a hotel at the Car Show."

"That sounds lovely," said Mrs Montague.

"Monstrous!" said Wilf.

"Er … yeah. Monstrous," said Maud. Out of the frying pan and into the fire! Now, not only did she have to write a perfect essay, she had to spend all holiday trying to keep the truth about the Wild family from her parents. This was shaping up to be the least relaxing break ever.

The clouds parted, and the car park was bathed in bright moonlight. Maud looked up at the waxing moon. By the time of the holiday, it would be full.

A camping holiday with a pack of werewolves.

During a full moon.

Perfect.

Chapter Four

Milly was grumbling again. "Where are my heart-shaped sunglasses?" she shouted. "How am I supposed to go camping without my heart-shaped sunglasses?"

Maud fished her torch out of the mess on the floor. Her half of the bedroom was a tangle of dirty clothes, monster masks and insect jars, while her sister's half was spotless, with everything tidied into her chest of drawers. But somehow Maud always seemed to find her things more easily. She'd already packed her exercise book, pens, waterproof, magnifying glass and *Spotter's Guide to Worms and Bugs*, while Milly was still flapping around looking for her sunglasses.

"This is going to be the worst holiday in the history of the world," said Milly. "I can't believe we've got to go camping with your weirdo friends."

"Would you rather go to the Classic Car Show?" asked Maud.

"No, I'd rather go to Corfu," said Milly. "Like Mum and Dad promised. I can't believe I won't be able to sunbathe. I won't even get to build a pretty sandcastle."

Maud was glad about that. Last time they'd gone to the beach, Milly had spent all day working on a perfect replica of Dream Castle from her favourite *Pink Pony Princess Party* book. Meanwhile Maud had recreated the castle from *Dracula*, with some help from Quentin in his vampire-rat costume.

Honk! Honk!

Maud stuck her head out of the window and saw her dad's car approaching. He was towing a large, battered lump of metal. Maud squinted at it. Was that a caravan? It was peppered with dents and scratches. The side panels were probably meant to be white, but they'd picked up so much grime they were now a dingy grey. Tattered beige curtains hung behind cracked and dusty windows.

Mr Montague turned into the driveway and the caravan followed, tottering on its rickety wheels.

"You'll never believe it," he called up, getting out of the car. "I found this in the scrapyard. The things people throw away!"

Maud could easily believe he found it in the scrapyard. What she couldn't believe was that he hadn't left it there.

Milly joined Maud at the window.

"What do you think?" asked Mr Montague.

"I think you should let me stay in a hotel as a

reward for doing well in my exams," said Milly. "Then you and Mum will have more space in the caravan."

"That's very thoughtful of you," said Mr Montague. "But there are no hotels near Oddington Marshes. Tell you what though, you can stay in the tent. Your mum's almost managed to get that funny smell out of it."

"Come on, girls!" Mrs Montague called from downstairs. "Time to go!"

"Well, this is already a disaster," Milly grumbled to Maud, as she shut the window. "I can't find my sunglasses and I'm going to have to sleep in that smelly, leaky old tent."

Maud put her backpack on and went downstairs. On the way out, she popped into the garage and scooped Quentin into the front pocket of her waterproof.

"Sorry this isn't as comfortable as my blazer," she said. "But I've stuffed the bottom with cotton wool. Hope it helps."

Quentin burrowed into the cotton wool, looked up and gave a ratty smile. *At least someone likes their holiday accommodation*, thought Maud.

She went outside and waited in the car.

Her parents wheeled their cases down the driveway. Instead of their usual matching raincoats, they were both wearing brand new leather jackets. With their thick, round glasses, they looked like they belonged to a gang of biker librarians.

"What are you wearing?" asked Maud.

"Oh, these?" her dad said. "I just picked them up in the sales. Pretty cool, huh?" He flipped up the jacket's collar and winked.

Maud didn't think they were very cool at all. Even the word 'cool' didn't sound cool when her dad said it.

"You're not copying Wilf's parents, are you?" asked Maud.

"Of course not," said Mr Montague. "Chill out! You're messing up my vibe."

Maud buried her face in her hands.

Milly dragged her case into the car and slumped on the back seat. "Come on, then. Let's get this over with."

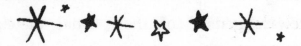

Her dad checked his mirrors, clicked his fingers and said, "Let's roll." He was about to turn his key in the ignition when something that looked like a small black rubber ball bounced off the back window.

"What was that, dear?" asked Mrs Montague.

Maud looked out. Paprika was lying on the ground with his cape crumpled over his head.

"Just a minute," she said. "I'll deal with this."

She got out quickly, dragged Paprika into the

neighbour's driveway and propped him against the fence while he got his breath back.

"What on earth are you doing?" she hissed. "I told you not to come here in bat form. What if my parents had seen you change?"

"Sorry," said Paprika. "I'm still trying to get the hang of transforming and landing at the same time. But I came to warn you. Don't go camping with Wilf and his family. You'll be in terrible danger!"

Mr Montague stuck his head out of the window. "Come on, dude!" he called. "We need to burn some rubber."

"It's Paprika from my class," said Maud. "I'm just telling him about our … uh … homework." She lowered her voice and whispered to Paprika. "Is this because of the full moon?"

"Sort of," he said. "But there's something else. What do you know about Oddington Marshes?"

"Nothing much,' said Maud. "Wilf says it's a nice campsite, but the facilities are a little basic." Paprika shuddered.

"What's wrong with it?" asked Maud.

"The Beast of Oddington lives there," said Paprika in a low voice. "You must have heard of it. It's the most terrifying creature for miles around. Even monsters are scared of it."

Maud tried to imagine what sort of beast could frighten vampires, ghosts and zombies.

"I'm sorry," said Maud. "It's too late to cancel it now."

"Please," said Paprika, reaching out to Maud with his trembling hand. "Don't go!"

"I've got to," Maud said. She turned her back on Paprika and walked back to the car. She could hardly tell her parents there was a monster without revealing the rest of the truth about Rotwood.

"Alright, let's do this," said Mr Montague, as

Maud slammed her door shut. He stuck in a CD called *Wild at Heart – Ultimate Driving Hits*.

"Excuse me," said Milly. "But I've brought my *Pink Pony Princess Party* CD. I think we'd all rather listen to that."

But it was no use. Both Maud's parents were already singing along to 'Born to be Wild' in fake American accents.

At last they drove off.

In the rear-view mirror, Maud could see Paprika waving. He looked terribly sad. Almost as if he were waving goodbye for the very last time.

Chapter Five

$\mathcal{M}$r Montague stopped the car, and the caravan creaked to a halt behind them. They had come to the end of a narrow country lane with thick hedges on either side. In front of them was a rusty iron gate. It was buckling outwards, as if something had tried to escape and failed. Beyond, Maud could see a clump of leafless black trees growing from boggy ground. A crow cawed, somewhere in the distance.

Maud tried to look on the bright side. At least the journey was over. That meant no more 'Born to be Wild' and no more stories about pink ponies having parties. Whatever horror lay beyond those gates, it couldn't be worse than that.

"This can't be our campsite," said Milly. "There's no spa. There's no heated pool. I can't even see any shops."

"It does look at bit run-down," said Mrs Montague. "Are you sure we're in the right place?"

"I hardly think my Sat Nav would lie to me," said Mr Montague.

He pressed a button on the black box, and a robotic female voice said, "You have reached your destination. Please watch out for potholes, fallen trees, marshland, swamps, flash flooding, insect attack …"

Mr Montague switched the machine off quickly.

"Yep," he said. "We're in the right place. Could one of you girls get the gate?"

"I'll do it," said Maud. She hopped out,

squelched across the ground and dragged the rusty bolt aside. The gate creaked open. A muddy track led into dense fog between the hedges. Maud's dad drove in, and Maud closed the gate again.

After she'd climbed back into the car, they continued down a track riddled with overgrown roots and fallen branches. A sign nailed to one of the trees read:

"Well, that settles it!" said Mr Montague cheerfully. "We're in the right place."

"You have to be joking," said Milly. "I want to go home right this instant."

"I think Milly might be right," said Maud.

"It does say to keep out."

"Don't be such a square," said Mr Montague. "Where's your sense of adventure?"

It felt as though they were driving over a never-ending cattle grid. Behind them, the caravan bounced up and down and leaned from side to side, threatening to tip over and take them with it.

"If they don't even have a proper road," said Milly, "I'm pretty sure they won't have a proper pool."

Maud lifted Quentin out of her pocket so he could look out of the window. Mist was snaking around dead trees and thick clumps of nettles.

"So this is Oddington," said Maud. "What do you think?"

Quentin's fur stood on end.

"Yeah, me too," said Maud.

Suddenly, there was a high-pitched howl from deep in the woods. Milly squealed. Quentin burrowed deep into Maud's pocket, his back legs kicking up small tufts of cotton wool. Mr Montague slammed his foot on to the brake. He peered into the fog ahead of them and checked his mirrors.

"I don't know why anyone would walk their dog in this weather," he said, driving slowly on.

The mist thinned out as the car spluttered on to smoother ground. They emerged in a clearing of flat, firm earth with a few tree stumps dotted about. It was surrounded by thick woodland on each side, and sloped down to a deep swamp.

Maud's dad let out a sigh of relief as Mr Wild's red truck appeared in front of them. "See?" Mr Montague said. "Nothing to worry about. We've arrived!"

Warren and Wilf were tossing a tennis ball back and forth, catching it in their mouths.

Mr Montague parked at the far end of the

clearing, and Maud jumped out of the car and rushed over.

"Hi, Mau – oof!" said Wilf.

Warren had let the tennis ball drop to the floor and grabbed Wilf in a headlock.

"Grrrr!" said Warren.

Wilf pulled at Warren's forearm and scrabbled his feet around. "Let me go!"

"Only when you admit you're the weakest little brother in the whole world," growled Warren.

"Stop it!" said Maud. "I don't know why you're showing off. There's no one here to watch."

"I was enjoying it, actually," said a mocking voice that Maud knew all too well. Poisonous Penelope stepped out of a ragged black tent at the edge of the clearing.

Penelope was a witch with straggly purple hair and a pointed hat, and she was Maud's least favourite classmate. She was wearing black wellingtons and a waterproof version of her usual black dress. "Hello, Montague," she said.

"What are you doing here?" asked Maud.

"I'm Warren's best friend," said Penelope. "I always come. I'm surprised Wilf managed to find a friend this year, too. He's so totally un-monstrous."

Mr and Mrs Wild strode out into the clearing, wearing matching red wellingtons and checked shirts. "Glad you could all make it," said Mr Wild. He turned to his fighting sons and let out a low, angry growl. Maud thought he was going to tell Warren off, but instead he said, "I've told you before, Wilf. You need to throw your weight to get out of a headlock. And stop whining."

Maud picked up the tennis ball and threw it over Warren's head. "Fetch," she said.

Warren's eyes followed it, and he bounded off, releasing Wilf.

"Good boy," said Maud.

"Fight your own battles next time," said Mr Wild, pointing his finger at Wilf. "You shouldn't need little girls to help you."

"Sorry, Dad," said Wilf, rubbing his neck.

Mr Wild stomped back over to his truck.

"I'm glad you're here," said Wilf.

"That's alright," said Maud. "My parents are excited about it. I think they really like your mum and dad."

She pointed to her dad, who had untethered the caravan and was now chatting to Mr Wild. He was saying words like 'awesome' and 'groovy', and making Mr Wild cringe.

"I'd better put my tent up," said Maud. "Where's yours?"

"We don't have any," said Wilf.

"You came camping without a tent?" asked Maud, surprised.

"Of course," said Wilf. "Why hide under a tent when you could be out in the open, feeling the moonlight on your fur?"

Maud gulped. Keeping the truth about the Wilds' secret from her parents was going to be even harder than she'd thought.

She headed back to the car, where Milly was still sitting in the back with her seatbelt on and her arms folded.

"Fancy helping me with the tent?" asked Maud.

"No," said Milly. "I fancy getting out of this mud pit right now, and I'd like to know why no one is listening to me."

"I'm sure you'll find something to do," said Maud. "Maybe you could build a swamp-castle."

Milly ignored her, so Maud went round to the boot and hauled out the tent. She dragged it into the middle of the clearing and tested the ground with her finger. It was firmer than the surrounding bog, but it was still squidgy. At least it would be easy to get the pegs in.

As Maud unrolled the tent, Wilf ran to the other side and grabbed a corner. He stretched it over the ground and pushed a peg into the soil.

"Is your dad always so harsh?" asked Maud as they worked.

"He's usually much worse," said Wilf, clicking two of the poles together. "He thinks all wolves should be fierce and strong. He's proud of Warren, but he says I'm so nice I couldn't even frighten a postman. I wish there was something I could do to convince him that I'm a big bad wolf."

Maud crawled inside the tent and shoved the poles upright. "I'll try and help if you like, as soon as I've written my essay."

"That would be monstrous!" said Wilf, stretching the waterproof flysheet over the top.

Maud got out and pulled the rope at the front until it was taut.

"Thanks, Wilf," she said. "I think that tent's staying put now."

Just then, a violent gust of wind blew through the clearing, parting the wisps of mist. It lifted the tent straight up into the air, where it flew around like a huge kite, until finally plummeting into the stagnant bog at the bottom of the slope.

"Drat," said Maud.

As she padded down to the bog and grabbed the corner of her soggy tent, she heard a cackle coming from behind her. Penelope was watching from the clearing, grinning.

"How do you like my holiday reading?" she asked, holding up a dusty hardback book called *Weather Spells for Beginners*. "I'm only on the first chapter and it's going down a storm. Literally." She broke into another fit of giggles.

"Hilarious," said Maud, dragging her muddy tent back up the slope.

"Wilf told me you need to get full marks on your essay or you'll drop down a year," said

Penelope with mock concern. "You know how much I'd hate to see you get thrown out of our class. But it's not going to be easy with all this unpredictable weather around."

Maud said nothing, but she knew Penelope was right. Writing a flawless Fright essay would be difficult at any time. But with a witch playing magical pranks on her, it was going to be practically impossible.

Chapter Six

Mr Montague clapped his hands together. "There we are!" he said. "It's going a treat now!"

Maud's dad had finally managed to get a small fire going after almost an hour of searching for dry twigs in the soggy swamp. The Wilds and the Montagues sat around on canvas stools, while weak flames and sparks flickered into the night air.

Only Milly had refused to join in. She'd dashed straight from the car to the caravan, and announced she was going to stay inside and alphabetise her flower-pressing collection until the whole 'ordeal' was over.

"Who knows a good campfire song?" asked Mr Montague.

"I know 'Born to be Wild'," said Mrs Montague hopefully.

"That's not a campfire song," said Maud. "If anything, that's a driving song. And I think we've all heard it enough for one day."

Maud turned to her exercise book and started to scribble.

The Fright of My Life
By Maud Montague

My biggest fright was the time I almost ate a dead woodlouse. I put it in my lunchbox for safekeeping. But then I forgot and when I opened it again, I thought it was a raisin.

Maud looked back at her essay. She'd just started and she could already tell it wasn't going to be nearly frightening enough. She ripped the page out of her book and threw it into the fire.

"Thank you kindly," said Mr Montague. "Every little helps."

Maud thought she'd be making a lot of kindling at the rate she was going. Everything she wrote seemed wrong. Thinking up scary stuff was harder than it sounded.

Mrs Wild unzipped her picnic bag and brought out a packet of raw steaks. "I hope everyone's hungry," she said. "It's time for dindins!"

Warren barked with excitement as Mrs Wild tore into the packet with her teeth and handed out the steaks.

"My, do those look good," said Mrs Montague. "How are we going to cook them?"

"Cook them?" asked Mr Wild. "And take all the flavour out?"

He chomped off the end of the raw steak and chewed it noisily. Mrs Wild and Warren did the same.

Maud waited for her parents to cry out with disgust, but they both kept smiling politely.

The sight of the Wilds gnashing away with flecks of blood on their strong white teeth was pretty ghastly. But they were werewolves, and Maud supposed it was the natural way for them to eat. Anyway, lots of humans ate in very odd ways. Milly always refused to eat her dinner unless it was chopped into little bits and colour coded on her special plate.

Wilf picked up his knife, fork and plastic plate, and started to cut up his raw steak. "Sorry about my family's table manners," he whispered to Maud. "We usually eat out of bowls on the kitchen floor."

"I heard that. And it's *your* manners you should be ashamed of," sneered Mr Wild with a half-chewed piece of steak in his mouth.

"You're in the woods, not a fancy restaurant."

Warren sniggered.

"Take no notice," whispered Maud. "You should eat your food whatever way you want."

Mrs Montague stared at her raw steak and nudged Mr Montague. "What should we do?" she asked quietly.

"We'd better join in," said Mr Montague, tearing a small piece off with his teeth. He chewed it a few times and swallowed it. "Excellent. Very rare. I think this is how the French eat it."

"Hmm," said Mrs Montague with a frown.

Mr Wild and Warren had already managed to finish their steaks. They both let out long, gurgling burps.

"I think I'll have mine well done," said Maud. She grabbed a skewer from the picnic basket and held the steak over the fire.

Maud watched the weak flames lap the meat and thought about her essay. She could remember plenty of scary events in her life, like the time she thought a branch tapping on her bedroom window was an escaped murderer, and the time her dad hired a clown for her fifth birthday, but none of them seemed frightening enough for full marks. Especially not in a school for monsters.

Mr Wild stood up and slapped his belly with satisfaction. "Time for a stroll. Fancy coming?"

"No, thanks," said Mr Montague, finishing his raw steak. He looked paler now, and was clutching his stomach. "I think I'll just turn in. Long day and all."

"A good jog can help the digestion, you know," said Mr Wild.

"No, really," said Mr Montague with a groan. "I could do with a bit of a lie down."

Mr and Mrs Wild shrugged and disappeared into the mist. Maud didn't believe they were going hiking so late at night, but she didn't want to think about what they were really up to.

"Try not to stay up too late," said Mr Montague. He trudged back to the caravan, followed by Mrs Montague, who quickly tucked her steak into the rubbish bag and fished a packet of peanuts out of her pocket. As soon as her parents opened the door, Maud could hear Milly whining. Even though her tent was caked with mud, she was glad she wasn't sharing the caravan with her sister.

Maud pulled her steak away from the fire and examined it. The edges were slightly browner, but it was still pretty much raw. This was going to take for ever.

Penelope grabbed a skewer and stuck her steak on the end of it. She wiggled her fingers, muttered under her breath, and fire whooshed around the meat, making it sizzle. She pulled out the skewer to reveal a perfect, well-done steak.

"Monstrous!" said Maud. "Will you do that to mine?"

"No, I don't think I will," said Penelope, taking a bite. "This really is excellent, though. Yum-yum-yum."

Maud didn't want Penelope to see she was jealous, so she concentrated on turning her own steak around in the meagre flames.

"That really was first class," said Penelope, when she'd finished. "Off to my nice, dry tent now. Good luck with the cooking."

On the other side of the campfire, Wilf was gathering the litter his family had tossed aside.

"Can I talk to you about something?" asked Maud.

"Sure," said Wilf. He tied a knot in the rubbish bag and sat down next to her.

"Paprika flew over to our house today," said Maud. "He came to warn me about something called the 'Beast of Oddington'. Have you ever heard of it?"

Wilf glanced around before leaning in. "There aren't many things that can scare us werewolves," he whispered. "But the Beast of Oddington is one of them. Even Dad's frightened of it. Everyone's told him he's mad to keep coming back here every year, but I think he's taken it as a challenge."

"So you've seen it?" asked Maud.

"No," said Wilf, "but last time we were staying here, we heard these strange howls in the night. And the next morning, there were giant scratch marks all down the truck."

"What sort of beast is it?" asked Maud.

"No one knows," said Wilf. "Nobody who's seen it has lived to tell the tale. But I've heard it has twenty-four eyes, long, sharp teeth and nostrils that breathe fire. And it must have pretty massive claws, judging from the scratches."

A twig snapped in the trees behind them. Maud and Wilf jumped up and spun around.

Maud could feel her heart beating faster as she peered into the murk. There seemed to be something moving.

"Roooaaaarrrr!"

Maud shrieked and Wilf yelped. Inside Maud's pocket, Quentin squeaked.

"H-h-hello?" said Maud. "Is anyone there?"

A figure emerged from the mist. It lurched closer and closer, until finally it stepped into the light of the campfire.

"Sorry," it growled. "Stubbed my toe."

Maud breathed a sigh of relief. It was just Warren.

A mocking laugh came from Penelope's tent. "Don't tell me you dweebs thought Warren was the Beast of Oddington?" she said.

"Of course not," said Maud. She sat down by the fire and held her steak over the flames again.

"Let me help with that," said Penelope.

Maud heard her muttering from over by her tent. It wasn't like the witch to be helpful, but Maud was so hungry she wasn't going to complain. She stared at her steak, waiting for the flames to engulf it.

There was a short clap of thunder and a tiny cloud appeared above the bonfire. A short, heavy shower pelted down on it, and within seconds the fire was out.

Penelope held up her copy of *Weather Spells for Beginners* and smirked. "Oh dear, I seem to have cast the wrong spell. Silly me!"

Warren grunted a guffaw.

Maud couldn't believe that witch. Playing nasty practical jokes was one thing, but now she had nothing to eat. "Why do you always have to be so mean?" she demanded.

Thunder cracked above them. Dark clouds swept in to join the tiny one above the campfire, and fat globs of rain started to fall. Maud lifted her hood over her head.

"That's enough, Penelope," said Wilf, lifting up his collar. "You're spoiling it for everyone."

"Don't be such a wimp," said Penelope. But she sounded unsure, and she glanced up at the clouds, which continued to thicken above them.

Warren growled at the sky and pulled the back of his jacket over the top of his head.

There was another loud clap, and the rain pelted down even harder. Within seconds, it had turned the mud into a watery swamp.

Maud leapt up as her canvas stool began sinking into the ground. Rain was running down her legs and into her wellies, and the front pocket of her jacket was filling up. Inside, Quentin had started practising his swimming.

"This isn't funny," said Maud. "Turn it off!"

Penelope looked up at the sky and down at her book. She wiped the rain off the pages and scanned through them.

The mud rose up the tyres of Mr Wild's car

and the front of Maud's tent.

"You don't know how to make it stop, do you?" asked Maud.

"Of course I do," said Penelope. "I just …"

There was a loud creak ahead of them. The mud was now so deep that the caravan was floating across it like a boat. The flowing slime was pushing it to the far end of the clearing.

"Quick!" shouted Maud. "My family's in there!"

"Uh-oh," said Wilf.

The caravan settled on the edge of the clearing for a moment, wobbling back and forth. With her heart in her mouth, Maud watched as a fresh wave of mud suddenly lapped up. The caravan began to slide down the treacherous slope to the swamp below.

Chapter Seven

Maud ran over, her feet sinking deeper into the mud with every step. She glanced over her shoulder. Wilf and Warren were squelching along behind her, followed by Penelope.

"Isn't there a spell to stop the rain?" yelled Maud.

"There was," said Penelope, "but the page is smudged and I can't read it." She flipped through the book as the rain lashed its pages. "Maybe I could try a different spell. I could summon a gust of wind to blow the caravan back up."

"No, no more spells! You'd probably blow them into the next village!" said Maud. "We'll have to rescue them ourselves."

At that moment, bright light flooded the clearing. Maud looked up to see a full moon shining between the rain clouds. At least it would be easier to see what they were doing now.

"Wilf, can you and your brother get around it and push it back up?" shouted Maud. "Wilf?"

There was no reply. Maud glanced over her shoulder and saw that the Wild brothers had both fallen to their hands and knees in the soupy mud. They looked up at the full moon and let out growls, as their jaws stretched and their arms and legs jutted back into awkward, impossible shapes. They craned their necks up as one and howled, with no trace of the human left in their voices.

Where the two boys had been standing, there were now a couple of wolves with thick brown coats, slobbering muzzles, and long, bushy tails. The smaller wolf barked and ran off into the mist. The larger wolf chased around in circles, trying to bite its own tail, before finally following.

"Come on," said Maud to Penelope. "We don't have any time to waste!"

Maud splashed on through the gloopy mud and reached the top of the slope, just as the back of the caravan was disappearing into the swamp. A rope tied to the tow bar was uncoiling in the slime in front of her. She grabbed hold of it, and Penelope grabbed on behind her.

"Some use those boys turned out to be," said Penelope through gritted teeth.

"They can't help it," said Maud breathlessly, her feet dragging through the mud like a water-skier. "Wilf can't think straight when he's in wolf form. He once chased a squirrel for thirty miles and had to call his dad to pick him up."

"I might have known you'd stick up for that pathetic puppy," said Penelope. "It's hardly surprising, given that you've only got two friends."

"That's still twice as many as you," said Maud.

No matter how much they pulled, it was no use. The caravan was still falling deeper and deeper into the swamp.

Maud looked around desperately and spotted a thick tree-stump sticking out of the mud. She stretched the rope as far as it would go. It was just long enough to loop once around the stump. She tied it in a double knot, hoping it would hold.

The rope twanged tight. Maud held her breath … and the caravan halted.

Maud breathed a huge sigh of relief. The bog was covering the bottom half of the caravan door. She wouldn't be able to rescue her family just yet, but at least they were safe.

She looked across the clearing to the spot she'd pitched her tent. Through the slanting rain, she saw it sink down into the mud with a loud glug.

"Drat!" said Maud.

Penelope chuckled with glee, the rain pouring off her hat.

There was a squelch from the other side of the clearing, as the witch's black tent collapsed into the mud, too.

Penelope's laughter tailed off.

"Well, I hope you enjoyed your joke, at least," said Maud.

"I was just trying to lighten things up," said Penelope. "I didn't know it would rain so much."

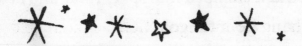

Maud scanned the clearing. The ground was so soggy, it would swallow her up if she tried to sleep on it. The only solid surface around was the roof of the caravan.

She sighed, waded through the mud and clambered up the front of the vehicle on to the roof, followed by Penelope. The rain was easing off now, but a cold wind blew through Maud's soaked clothes, making her shiver.

"Well, this is just perfect," said Penelope.

"And whose fault is that?" asked Maud.

"Alright," said Penelope. "There's no need to go on about it."

She took her hat off and laid it on its side to make a pillow. Within a few seconds, she was snoring loudly.

Maud took Quentin out of her pocket and tried to dry him with a tissue. His fur was so wet, it had clumped into spiky tufts, and he was shivering from the cold.

"You poor thing," said Maud. "I'm afraid we're not going to get much warmer tonight." The roof of the caravan was curved, and it was impossible to find a comfortable spot, but Maud stretched out as best she could. She looked up at the bright moon. The caravan was stuck in the bog, her tent was under the mud, and the Wilds were dashing around on all fours. And this was just the first night.

So far, the holiday was off to a horrible start.

Chapter Eight

Maud hurtled through the woods, crunching black leaves and scrabbling over dead branches. The Beast was closing in on her, its foul breath warm on her neck. She heard its razor-sharp claws swish through the air, terrifyingly close to her head.

Maud stumbled. She tried to find her footing again, but it was too late. She was falling, easy prey for the vicious monster. She looked back just in time to see it open its slimy jaws.

"Wakey-wakey," it said, in a strangely sweet voice. "Come on, sleepyhead."

It sounded an awful lot like her dad. Maud opened her eyes.

Mr Montague was leaning out of the window of the caravan, shielding his eyes from the bright morning sun. "Must have been quite the storm last night, eh?"

"Don't tell me you slept through it," said Maud.

"I did get a sort of slipping sensation at one point," said Mr Montague. "But I assumed it was indigestion."

Milly stuck her head out of the window. She had bags under her eyes, and her hair was coated with pressed flowers.

"Well, I hardly slept at all," she said, scowling. "There was a horrid, howling noise all night. And I dreamt huge swamp-slugs were crawling over the roof. It turns out I wasn't far wrong."

Penelope sat up and rubbed her eyes. She pressed the dent out of her hat and put it on.

"What a wonderful night," she said. "We must do it again sometime!"

Mr Montague craned his head round to look up towards the campsite.

"Well done for tying us to the tree," he said. "Very resourceful, dear." He clambered out of the window and leapt down into the mud, shouting out, "Geronimo!" Then he squelched his way up to dry ground and grasped hold of the rope. "I hope you're all ready for tug o' war!"

Maud scrambled down from the roof and lined up behind him. Penelope climbed down too, but wandered straight past.

Mrs Montague followed Mr Montague through the window. "Out you get, Milly," she shouted. "We've all got to muck in."

Milly shook her head. "I'm not going near any muck. The only time I'm going to set foot out of here is when we're safely home."

"Oh, never mind," said Mr Montague. "She doesn't weigh much, anyhow."

Mrs Montague took her place behind Maud and gripped the rope.

"On the count of three, everybody pull!" said Mr Montague. "One … two … three … heave!" Maud tugged the rope with all her strength. The caravan budged an inch and then slurped back into the sticky mud.

"Let's try again," said Mr Montague, wiping a bead of sweat from his forehead. "One … two … three … heave!"

This time the caravan crept up a couple of inches before sliding down again.

"Okay," said Mr Montague, panting hard. "Nearly there."

Mr Wild padded over to them, looking fresh as a daisy. "Morning, friends. Need a hand?"

"Sure, dude," said Mr Montague. "That would be awesome."

Mr Wild raised a bushy eyebrow and grabbed the rope.

"One … two … three … heave!" shouted Mr Montague.

Mr Wild casually pulled the rope with one

hand, dragging the caravan out of the swamp and sending Maud and her parents crashing to the ground.

Mr Montague stood up and wiped the mud from his hands. "Thanks everyone," he wheezed. "Good … er … team effort."

Maud got to her feet and climbed back up into the clearing. The mud had set in the morning sun. Maud could see her footprints from the night before, now formed into deep craters. Further away were Warren's and Wilf's tracks, which became paw prints as they transformed and bounded off into the forest. Maud might have been worried – but thankfully, her parents never noticed anything.

Then she spotted that there was another row of tracks beyond those of the Wild brothers. Maud went over to examine them.

She gasped. They'd been made by something about three times the size of a human foot. At the front were four long talons that tapered to razor-thin points. They looked like a dinosaur's footprint she'd seen once in a museum.

Maud shuddered to think that whatever made these prints had passed so close to her while she slept.

"Look at this," shouted Penelope. She was standing behind Mr Wild's truck, which was listing to one side. "Here's something you won't be able to blame on me."

Maud raced over and looked at the tyres. Something had ripped them apart in neat, parallel slashes.

"Not again!" shouted Mr Wild. He kicked the side of his truck and let out a terrifying roar. "It took me ages to fix it last time."

He went to kick the truck again, but Mrs Wild held him back. "That's not going to help, dear," she said.

Mr Montague picked up a scrap of shredded rubber. "How very strange," he said. "But not to worry. I can drive you to a garage and pick up some replacements if you like."

"That's very kind of you," said Mrs Wild.

"I'll stay and keep an eye on the little ones," said Mrs Montague.

"Great," said Mr Montague. He took a pair of clip-on sunglasses from his top pocket and clipped them on to the bridge of his glasses. Maud thought it made him look like a giant bug. "Let's hit the highway!"

Mr and Mrs Wild exchanged a glance and climbed into the car.

Mr Montague started up the engine, and Milly stuck her head out of the caravan window. "Brilliant! Are we going now?"

"Not yet, petal," answered Mr Montague. "We're off to find a garage. We'll be back soon." He stuck 'Born to be Wild' in the CD-player, and they set off down the track.

Milly rolled her eyes, before slamming the window so hard the caravan wobbled.

"I'll go and check on her," said Mrs Montague. "The rest of you play nicely."

"What do you think happened to the tyres?" asked Maud.

"Isn't it obvious?" said Penelope. "It was the Beast of Oddington."

Maud turned to see that Wilf and Warren had arrived back from their midnight romp, and were kneeling in the middle of the clearing, examining the clawprints. She wandered over to them.

"I can't believe the Beast of Oddington came through here last night," said Wilf. All his hair was standing on end.

"What should we do?" asked Penelope.

"I packed a couple of fishing rods in the

truck," said Wilf. "We could go down to the lake, if you like."

"I'd love to," said Penelope. "But I've just remembered that fishing is totally lame."

"I should get on with my essay," said Maud sadly.

Penelope yawned. "Or we could do something completely monstrous instead. Like catching the Beast of Oddington."

Maud looked at Penelope in surprise. Catch the Beast? That could make a great essay. Maybe even one good enough to get full marks …

"That sounds fun," said Wilf, his voice wavering. "But I think I'd still rather go fishing."

"Just as I thought," sneered Penelope. "The little puppy's too frightened to come. Poor little bow-wow. Is he going to make a puddle on the floor when he sees the scary Beast?"

Maud made up her mind. "I bet we can find the Beast before you," she said.

Penelope laughed. "Watch out, Beast of

Oddington!" she said. "The loser patrol is on its way! You're on!"

She and Warren set off into the forest.

"Well, now that we're rid of them," said Wilf, "let's go get the fishing rods!"

Maud looked from the woods to Wilf, unsure. "I don't know," she said. "I didn't want to hang around with Warren and Penelope, but that doesn't mean I don't want to look for the Beast. Just imagine if we discovered it first. What an adventure that would be! You'd convince your dad you're just as brave as Warren, and I'd get something to write my essay about."

Wilf looked down at his feet. "Maybe if I caught a big fish instead. One with a really stern expression. That would still be quite brave, wouldn't it?"

"Not really," said Maud. "Being brave means forcing yourself to do things you don't want to do. It means pushing yourself on, even when part of you resists."

Wilf was silent for a moment. Then he looked up and said, "Alright. Let's do it!"

"Monstrous!" said Maud. She held her hand up for a high-five, and Wilf gave it a weak slap.

There was no turning back now. They had to find the Beast, and they had to do it before Penelope did.

Chapter Nine

The sun had gone in, and wisps of mist were descending again, making the forest look scary ... but exciting, too. They followed the tracks out of the clearing and among the leafless black trees. Then Maud noticed something strange about the prints – they were completely identical and spaced evenly in a straight line.

"Weird," said Maud. "Does the Beast hop along on one leg?"

Wilf shrugged. "I've never seen it."

They pressed on, deeper into the forest. The mist grew thicker with every step they took.

Soon it was so thick that Maud could barely see a few feet ahead of her. She stepped over thick roots and ducked under low branches, keeping her eyes on the trail. Then she heard a sudden howl – low and mournful – echoing through the trees. She felt a trembling in the pocket of her coat.

"Don't worry, Quent," said Maud. "It's probably just Warren stubbing his toe again."

"It doesn't sound like him," said Wilf. "In fact, it doesn't sound like a human or a wolf. We ought to go back now. Maybe we could look for the Beast later, when the mist clears?"

"No," said Maud, trying to sound brave. "This proves we're close. We have to keep going."

The forest grew even thicker, and Maud could barely see ten paces ahead. The black branches of the trees meshed so close to her head that it felt as though she was walking down a crooked corridor. She cried out as her knee bumped into something, and she stumbled forward. It was the trunk of an overturned tree. At first Maud thought last night's storm might have pushed it over, but after looking closer she knew that wasn't right. It had been ripped apart at the base. Huge gashes streaked the bark, and splinters the size of daggers were strewn across the ground. Something very strong had destroyed that tree. Very strong ... and very angry.

Sharp bursts of pain shot into Maud's arm as Wilf grabbed her. "Ouch! Your claws are out!"

"Sorry," said Wilf. "Look! There's something in the grass!" He pointed to a patch of tall weeds.

Maud peered into the undergrowth. When she realised what she was looking at, she walked over and bent down to pick it up.

"It's not a beast," she said, smiling. "But I think it might help us find one."

She wiped the grime from the cover of the

eather book. It was Penelope's *Weather Spells for Beginners.*

"Penelope must have dropped it!" said Wilf.

Maud flipped through the book. Some of the pages were damaged from the downpour the night before, but she could still see a snow spell, a rainbow spell and a spell to banish mist. What luck!

Maud glanced at the words etched on the back. "No wand or training required," it read. "Just say the rhyme and change the clime. So simple even an ogre could make it work." She flipped to a page headed "Mist Banishment Spell by Malicious Mildred, aged 105".

Pointing towards the thick fog ahead, she began to read:

"Mist be gone away from me,
Clear my path so I can see,
I banish you with all my might,
Move aside and end my plight."

Maud wiggled her fingers, and the mist evaporated in front of them, revealing bare black trees. She moved her hand around, and the mist fell away, as if she were aiming a gigantic leaf-blower.

"Monstrous!" said Wilf.

Maud smiled and walked on, pointing her hand downwards so she could follow the huge prints. They led around an oozing swamp and a large patch of straggly reeds, and came to an abrupt halt at the edge of a clump of dark green pine trees.

"Where could the Beast have gone?" asked Maud.

"Maybe it's here," said Wilf, glancing nervously around. "Maybe it's hiding in those trees."

Maud listened, but there was complete silence.

"I don't think so," said Maud. "I'm sure we'd be able to hear something."

"Maybe the Beast can fly," said Wilf. "Maybe this is the spot it took off from."

Maud pointed her hand upwards. She held her breath, imagining the glinting talons she might uncover. But the mist flew away to reveal an empty sky.

Wilf got down on his hands and knees and sniffed the ground.

"There's a scent over here," he said.

Following Wilf's nose, Maud found a new set of tracks leading into the pine trees, but they were much smaller than the beastly footprints they'd been following.

"These are shoeprints," said Maud. "Could Penelope and Warren have got ahead of us?"

Wilf stuck his nose into one of them and inhaled. "No, it doesn't smell as bad as my brother."

"Then we need to find whoever made them,

and fast," said Maud. "They probably have no idea of the danger they're in."

Wilf padded alongside the prints, picking out a path through the pine cones and fallen needles. Maud followed, blasting the fog out of their way. Wilf actually seemed to be enjoying the hunt now. His dad would have been proud.

The prints led them to a gap in the trees. Maud caught her breath. In front of them, a neat stone path wound through a bed of red and pink roses to the door of a small white cottage. It was clean and well kept, with a thatched roof and a trellis in front covered with bright yellow flowers. Maud thought it looked like a pretty holiday home, but what was it doing in the middle of this bleak, desolate swamp?

Chapter Ten

*P*lumes of sweet-smelling smoke rose up from the stone chimney.

"Looks like someone's in," said Maud. "We'd better go in and warn them about the Beast."

Maud dashed up the path. She clacked a large bronze doorknocker and soon heard someone shuffling slowly around inside.

The door creaked open, and an old lady emerged. She was wearing a soft, white dressing gown with pink, fluffy slippers, and had thin, white hair curled neatly around her head. She peered down at Maud and Wilf, her bright blue eyes made owlish by thick spectacles, and smiled warmly.

"Hello, dearies," she said. "What brings you out here?"

"We're camping," said Maud.

Maud thought she saw the woman's eyes narrow for an instant.

"How lovely, dear," said the woman, smiling broadly again.

"There's something we need to warn you about," said Wilf.

"Well, you'd better come in then," said the old lady. "I'm Mrs St John. Would you like a cup of tea and something to eat? I've scones, shortbread, chocolate fingers …"

"That sounds great," said Maud, her mouth watering. She felt she could eat several platefuls after the previous night's cookery disaster.

Mrs St John led them through a bright hallway with a wooden dresser and a large cupboard into a cosy kitchen with a low ceiling and an open fire. They sat down at an oak table, covered in placemats with watercolours of moles, badgers and hedgehogs on them. Mrs St John shuffled over to the sink and filled an old copper kettle.

"Monstrous!" said Wilf. "I love tea, but Dad doesn't like me drinking it. He says it's not wolfish enough."

"You'll have to bear with me," said Mrs St John, slapping the kettle on the stove. "I don't usually have guests round."

Maud wasn't surprised Mrs St John didn't get many visitors. It was a lonely and gloomy spot to live in, especially for a sweet old lady. Did she have to flee the Beast every time she popped out to the shops? And why weren't there bars on the windows or bolts on the doors?

"This is a very pretty house," said Maud. "How long have you lived here?"

"All my life," said Mrs St John. She took some scones out of her larder and arranged them on a plate. "My family's lived here for generations."

"Don't you get lonely?" asked Maud.

"Never," said Mrs St John. "Who'd want strangers poking around when you could have peace and quiet instead? All those ramblers and campers and yompers …" She was gripping a scone so tightly that it crumbled to pieces. "… trampling my flowerbeds … pitching their tents in my garden …"

Mrs St John looked at the crumbs in her hand and smiled again. "Present company excepted, of course. Silly me, I seem to have broken this scone! Let me fetch another one."

As Mrs St John went back to the larder, Wilf tapped Maud and pointed to a cupboard at the side of the room. Maud couldn't work out what he'd noticed. The door was open very slightly, but not enough to see inside. Then she spotted it. In front of the cupboard, there were a couple of muddy clawprints on the floor, just like the ones they'd been following.

"It smells just like the Beast's tracks! Do you think the monster's in there?" whispered Wilf.

"It can't be a very big monster if it is," said Maud. "It looks like there's barely room for an ironing board."

Mrs St John came over, plonked a plate of scones and chocolate fingers on the table, and returned to the stove. Maud looked from the cupboard back to the old lady, and all at once an idea occurred to her. *Could it be?* she wondered.

Maud lifted Quentin out of her pocket.

"I need you to do something," she whispered. "Run over to that cupboard and open the door." Quentin glanced at the huge clawprints and leapt straight back into Maud's pocket, pink legs kicking frantically.

Maud hauled him out again. "Don't worry," she whispered. "I'm sure the monster isn't in there. I think I might know what's going on, but I need you to help me prove it. There's a piece of scone in it for you."

Maud lowered Quentin to the floor, and he scuttled across as the kettle let out a high-pitched whistle.

"Do you take sugar?" asked Mrs St John.

"Yes, please," said Maud. "We'd both like four sugars."

Wilf turned to her and whispered, "But I don't usually have any sugar."

"Just trying to buy Quentin some time," muttered Maud.

Mrs St John poured four spoons of sugar into each cup and gave them a stir. She ambled over and placed the steaming cups on the table.

At that moment, the cupboard door flew open, and its contents spilled over the floor with a clatter. There was an ornate horn, a pair of strong metal shears, and an enormous cut-out in the shape of a claw.

Quentin darted back across the floor, scrabbled up the chair leg, and dived into Maud's pocket.

"Well done, Quent," said Maud. She broke off a piece of scone and handed it to him, then folded her arms and turned to the old lady. "So, what's all that stuff doing in your cupboard, Mrs St John?" she said. "Or should I say ... the Beast of Oddington!"

Chapter Eleven

Mrs St John gave a gasp. "I'm sure I don't know what you mean!" she said, scrabbling around on her hands and knees to scoop everything back inside the cupboard.

"Don't give me that," said Maud. "That's the very clawprint we've been following from our campsite. It's even got an elastic strap on the back, to put your foot through. And those shears look exactly the right size to make the scratch marks we've seen and slash tyres!"

"Yeah," said Wilf. "And I don't even take sugar in my tea."

Maud wasn't quite sure why that mattered, but at least Wilf was trying to help.

Giving up, Mrs St John let everything fall to the floor. She got to her feet.

"Alright, I admit it," she said fiercely. "I am the Beast of Oddington."

"Ah-hah!" cried Wilf, hopping to his feet. Then a look a confusion crossed his face. "Wait … really?"

"Why do you want everyone to think there's a monster here?" asked Maud.

"To save Oddington," said the old woman, gesturing all around her. "This is such a quiet, lovely spot. I don't want strangers trampling all over it."

Maud and Wilf gave each other a sidelong glance. Quiet maybe, but lovely?

"What's it to you if a few harmless ramblers pass through?" asked Maud.

"You don't understand," cried Mrs St John. "One day, years ago, some men in hard hats and neon jackets called round here. They showed me some blueprints. Said they were building a holiday camp with a pool and a spa and an unlimited buffet."

Mrs St John was spitting the words out, a blue vein on her pale forehead bulging.

"I had to stop them. Oddington has always been such a peaceful place. I couldn't bear to think about all those loud, chubby families stomping around."

"There must have been someone you could go to," said Maud. "My dad launched a petition last year. I think it was to stop the city centre from being pedestrianised."

"I tried," said Mrs St John. "I wrote to the council, but they said it was too late. I was about to throw the letter away when I noticed that they'd misspelled my name. I'm Bea, you see, short for Beatrice. Bea St John. And they'd written 'Beast John'. At first I thought, *How rude!* But it gave me the idea."

"But how did you do it?" asked Wilf. "What were all those spooky noises?"

Mrs St John picked up the horn and blew into it. A low howl blasted out.

"I ran around leaving clawprints and blowing the horn whenever the mist came down," said Mrs St John. "Soon word of the horrendous Beast spread, and all the yompers and campers stayed away. Even the builders abandoned the place eventually. I listened to the blissful peace and quiet, and I knew I'd done the right thing."

"It was certainly clever," said Wilf. "But I don't think you should have slashed Dad's tyres."

The old lady slumped into an armchair and put her head in her hands.

"Please don't tell anyone," she pleaded. "All I wanted was to preserve Oddington. Wouldn't you have done the same to save your home?"

Maud looked out of the window. Oddington was sort of pretty, if you ignored the mist, marshes and dead trees. If they walloped a holiday camp in the middle of it, a coffee shop would soon follow, then a supermarket, then a bowling alley. Soon it would be concreted over like so many other places, and all the spookiness would be gone forever. She thought about all the crazy things she'd done to make sure Rotwood stayed safe, and made up her mind.

Just as she was about to speak, Maud spotted movement among the trees outside. She got up and peered out of the window. Penelope and Warren were bumbling through the mist towards the house.

"Alright," said Maud. "Your secret is safe with us. But you must help us with something."

Mrs St John looked up. "Anything," she said. "Anything to keep my home the way it is."

Chapter Twelve

A minute later, Maud watched through a crack in the kitchen door as Mrs St John doddered down the hallway and opened the front door.

"Finally," said Penelope. "Do you know the way back to the clearing? We're lost."

"Certainly, dearies," said Mrs St John. "You walk back that way for ..."

Mrs St John looked behind Penelope and let out a terrified gasp. "Oh no! I just saw something in the trees! I think it was the Beast!"

Penelope spun around, her skin turning

pale. "What should we do?"

"Come inside," said Mrs St John, ushering them into the house. "You'll be safer in here."

Penelope and Warren darted inside, and Mrs St John slammed the door behind them.

Warren yelped with fear.

"Quiet!" barked Mrs St John. "Don't let it know you're afraid. It can smell fear."

"You don't think it will attack us, do you?" asked Penelope, her voice trembling.

"Attack you?" said the old lady. "It will do more than that. Last time it came round here it ate three children … whole. Nothing left of them but a pair of trainers and a sweet wrapper.'

Maud watched Penelope and Warren quaking with fright and tried not to giggle. She lifted the horn to the gap in the door and blew into it.

A deep howl filled the cottage, making the pictures in the hallway rattle.

"Good heavens! It's in the kitchen!" screamed

Mrs St John. "It must have come in through the back door!"

Penelope shrieked, and Warren whimpered.

"Shh!" hissed Mrs St John. "You'll draw it in here."

Maud sneaked over to the kitchen table, where she'd stored her scaring equipment. She wrapped the fluffy black bathroom rug around herself and tied it with elastic. She stuck wooden spoons into the ribbon on Mrs St John's summer hat and put it on. Then she attached forks to her fingers with rubber bands. Now she couldn't pick up the horn any more, so she bent down and grabbed it with her teeth, using her elbows to keep it steady.

She rushed back to the door as Mrs St John surreptitiously flicked the hall lights off.

"The power's gone!" yelled Mrs St John. "It's chewed through the cables! Saints preserve us!"

Maud flung the door aside, and Penelope and Warren screamed. In the dim light leaking in through the hall window, Maud saw them pressing their backs to the wall.

"It's the Beast!" shouted Mrs St John. "Look at its fearsome horns!"

Maud waggled her head, making the wooden spoons wobble from side to side.

"Look at its deadly claws!" cried Mrs St John.

Maud shook the forks attached to her fingers.

"Listen to its chilling roar!" said Mrs St John.

Maud blew the horn.

Penelope and Warren screamed again.

Just at that moment, Wilf burst in through the front door. "What's going on?"

"It's the Beast of Oddington! Run for your life!" shouted Penelope.

"Run? Never! I'll handle this," said Wilf, puffing his chest out. "You two hide in the cupboard."

Penelope and Warren rushed into the cupboard, and Wilf shut the door behind them. Mrs St John handed Wilf a cushion and a mop.

"Take that!" said Wilf. He bashed the mop into the cushion with a deep thud.

Maud blew the horn again. This time she tried to make it sound like an injured scream.

"Oh, you didn't like that did you?" asked Wilf. "Well, try this on for size."

Wilf hit the cushion again, and Maud tooted another short howl.

"You just don't quit, do you?" shouted Wilf. "Well, you've picked the wrong wolf to mess with this time!"

Wilf struck the cushion once more, and Maud let out a last, pained howl, before dashing back into the kitchen, trying as hard as she could to sound like a defeated beast fleeing into the woods.

When the door was shut behind her, Maud quickly took off her beast costume and hid it in a corner. From the hallway, she heard Wilf opening the cupboard and saying, "It's gone. And I don't think it will be back any time soon."

Maud opened the kitchen door and headed back into the hallway. "What happened? I heard something approaching, so I hid under the table."

"I fought the Beast of Oddington," said Wilf.

"Wow! You're a real hero! Thanks!" said Maud. "But what about Penelope and Warren. Didn't they help you?"

"No," said Wilf. "Actually, they hid in the cupboard."

"Yeah, thanks," muttered Penelope, looking down at the floor and shuffling awkwardly.

Mrs St John opened the front door and looked around. "You can go now. That brave young man scared the Beast off."

Warren and Penelope stepped out, glancing nervously around.

"That was monstrous!" Wilf told Mrs St John.

"Monstrous?" asked the old lady. "Is that the word you youngsters use these days? Yes, I suppose it was pretty monstrous, wasn't it? That girl with the purple hair got the fright of her life, and that fellow with her was the biggest wimp I've ever seen."

Maud giggled, then stopped suddenly. Hearing about Penelope getting the fright of her life reminded her she still hadn't started her essay. She didn't have much time left. But now she knew exactly what she was going to write about.

Chapter Thirteen

$\mathcal{W}$ilf's eyes shone. "It shot flames at me," he said. "But I didn't care. I just ducked to the side, leapt up and smacked it on the nose."

Maud and the Wild family were sitting around the spluttering campfire, listening to the story. Mr Wild was nodding as his son spoke, his eyes sparkling.

"Then it let out a scream of terror and raced off into the woods," Wilf continued. "It won't bother us again."

Mr Wild stood up and clapped Wilf on the shoulder. 'I'm proud of you, son. You did well.

Unlike your weakling of a brother."

"Sorry, Dad," said Warren, squirming. "You didn't see it, though. It was horrible."

"It was pretty fearsome," said Maud. "It's not surprising that Warren hid in the cupboard."

Mrs Wild shook her head and tutted. She took a packet of raw lamb chops out of her picnic bag and handed a couple to Wilf. "As a reward for being so brave, you can have your brother's supper, too."

"What am I going to eat?" cried Warren.

Mrs Wild took out a packet of bone-shaped dog biscuits and tossed them to him. He whimpered with shame, but tucked into them anyway.

Maud grinned and wandered over to the car, where her dad was wrestling their muddy tent into a black bin-bag.

"Are we off home?" Maud asked.

"Afraid so," said Mr Montague. "I don't want to risk sliding back into the swamp if the weather turns. Between you and me, I don't think this is very good terrain for camping. You need firm soil for pegs. Why they promote this place as a campsite I have no idea."

Maud was about to point out that a large 'KEEP OUT' sign hardly counted as encouragement, but she didn't want to be mean.

She noticed Penelope taking down her own tent, and headed over.

"I think this belongs to you?" she said, handing over Penelope's copy of *Weather Spells for Beginners*. "If only you hadn't dropped it. You might have been able to cast a spell at the Beast rather than running for the safety of the cupboard."

"It's not funny," said Penelope. She opened the book and pointed to a lightning-bolt spell. "And if you ever tell anyone about it, this is what you'll get."

"I promise I won't breathe a word," said Maud.

Penelope tramped back to the truck, where

Mrs Wild was loading the canvas stools into the boot.

Warren was waiting by the front door on the passenger side.

"Oh no, you don't," said Mr Wild. "Wilf gets the front seat today."

Warren opened the back door and skulked in.

Mr Wild started up the engine, and the truck rolled across the clearing on its huge wheels.

He passed Mr Montague, who was attaching the caravan to the back of the car, and honked his horn.

"Thanks for coming," he said. "Shame about the weather."

"That's summer for you," said Mr Montague, snorting out a laugh. "But thanks for inviting us all the same. Stay cool, dudes!"

Mr Wild forced a smile and sped away down the track. As they went, Warren stuck his head out of the back window and yapped mournfully.

Maud got in the back of their car. Milly was

sitting there with her flower-pressing book on her lap and her seatbelt on.

"So that's settled," Mrs Montague was saying. "We'll listen to our *Ultimate Driving Hits* collection until junction nine, and then we'll swap to your *Pink Pony Princess Party* CD.'

"Fine," said Milly. "As long as we get out of this place."

Maud didn't know which half of the journey she was looking forward to least, but she didn't really care. She had her exercise book, her pen and a very important essay to write.

As the car juddered away, with 'Born to be Wild' blaring out yet again, she opened her book and began again:

The Fright of My Life
By Maud Montague

Chapter Fourteen

Paprika was reaching the terrifying end of his story. "… And then they took it away and brought a salad instead," he read. He looked up from his exercise book and smiled at the class.

Maud was sitting at her desk in Mr Von Bat's class. Everyone else had read their Fright essays. Oscar had written about the time he accidentally dropped his head out of the car window and had to ask his dad to reverse and pick it up. Zombie Zak had told them about the time his jaw rotted off and he had to sew it back on. Finally, Paprika had described the time he'd been given garlic bread by mistake in a pizza restaurant.

"I remember it well," said Mr Von Bat. "It gave your mother a terrible headache, and I got yelled at all night. Seven out of ten."

Mr Von Bat turned to Maud. "Ah, Miss Montague, it looks as if we're left with you. Let's see how you got on. No pressure."

Maud stepped out to the front. She opened her exercise book and took a deep breath.

"The Fright of My Life. By Maud Montague." She cleared her throat. "My biggest ever fright was the time I saw the legendary Beast of Oddington."

There were gasps around the classroom. Billy Bones had been dragging his ruler up and down his ribs, but he put it down to listen. Oscar's head had been looking out of the window, but he grabbed it off the sill and turned it round to face Maud.

"It happened just a few days ago when I was on a camping trip with my friend Wilf Wild."

Wilf turned and waved at the class.

"We went out to Oddington Marshes, even though another good friend had warned me that a hideous creature haunts that lonely and desolate place."

Maud smiled at Paprika, who was looking terrified.

"One morning, we saw some giant clawprints leading away from our campsite. Wilf said we should follow them and find the monster. I was very scared, but Wilf was determined, so I gave in. We followed the clawprints through a foggy swamp and a dark forest until we came to a little white cottage. We knocked on the door, and an old lady called Mrs St John invited us inside. She had a roaring fire, a cosy kitchen, and a big cupboard at the end of the hallway."

Maud looked at the back of the room, where Penelope was glaring at her. *Weather Spells for Beginners* was sitting open on her desk.

"We were just having a nice cup of tea, when the front door was ripped right off its hinges and we heard a terrible roar. The hideous Beast of Oddington was upon us. It was the most fearsome thing I'd ever seen. It had long, sharp claws that looked a bit like forks, huge horns that looked sort of like wooden spoons, and a stomach that was as furry as a bathroom mat. It had twenty-four eyes, a row of long chomping teeth flecked with blood, and nostrils that spluttered out flames."

All around the class, pupils were leaning forward in their seats. Even Zombie Zak was paying attention, and he never seemed to follow what went on in lessons.

"I was so frightened that I screamed, ran into the cupboard and slammed the door behind me," said Maud.

Giggles erupted around the classroom.

"Lame," shouted Billy Bones.

"Chicken!" shouted a voice from the back of the room that must have been Invisible Isabel.

"Ug-Ug-Ug," grunted Zak, in what may have been a zombie chuckle.

Maud looked down at her exercise book again and continued to read. "I know that what I did was cowardly and stupid. I dashed for the nearest cupboard instead of facing the Beast. I am incredibly ashamed, and I now see how pathetic I was."

Maud looked over at Penelope, who was scowling.

"I am just lucky that Wilf was there," read Maud. "While I cowered in the cupboard, he attacked the monster. Thinking nothing of the Beast's swiping claws and snapping teeth, he ran forward and walloped it. The Beast backed off and came again, drool spilling between its black lips, and flames shooting from its nostrils. Wilf stood tall and struck it again. They fought long and hard, but in the end Wilf prevailed. The Beast let out a piercing cry and ran back into the forest."

Everyone in the class turned to look at Wilf, who shrugged casually.

"Seeing the Beast of Oddington gave me the fright of my life. I reacted like a scared little bunny rabbit, but thanks to Wilf's bravery, I'm here to tell the tale."

Maud closed her book, and the class applauded. Billy Bones and Zombie Zak got up to slap Wilf on the back. Only Penelope refused to join in.

"Settle down," said Mr Von Bat.

Maud returned to her seat. She watched Mr Von Bat intently, as he considered her essay. He rested his chin on his hands.

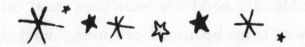

"Well, I don't think you behaved in a very monstrous fashion, Maud," he said. "Have all my Fright classes been for nothing?"

Maud's heart sank. It seemed as though all the effort she'd put in hadn't been enough.

"On the other hand, your essay was definitely very original," said Mr Von Bat. "And it certainly got the biggest reaction from the class. So I suppose I've got no choice but to give you full marks. Ten out of ten!"

"Monstrous!" shouted Maud, and her friends applauded all over again.

She was staying with her classmates!

Just then, the bell rang, and the other children leapt up from their desks and filed out of the classroom.

As Maud passed Mr Von Bat's desk on the way out, he beckoned her over. "Well done,

Montague," he said. "You might not have been very brave when you met the Beast, but at least you had the courage to admit it to the rest of us."

"Thank you, Sir," said Maud, grinning.

As she made her way over to the door, Penelope shoved past, stamping on her foot.

"Hey! I kept my promise, didn't I?" asked Maud. "I didn't mention you at all in my essay."

"I know you included all that stuff about the cupboard just to humiliate me," said Penelope. A nasty smirk spread across her lips. "But at least it means you'll be staying in our class. Where I can keep a close eye on you."

Penelope clutched her *Weather Spells for Beginners* to her chest and dashed off. Maud stepped into the hallway, where Wilf was signing his autograph on Zombie Zak's exercise book.

"Sign one of my ribs next," said Billy Bones, handing him a felt-tip.

"This is monstrous!" said Wilf. "I've never

had anyone think I was brave before."

Wilf scrawled his name on Billy's top rib and returned the pen.

"Cool," said Billy, rushing down the stairs. "I'm never going to bleach myself again."

Wilf saw Maud, raced over, and gave her a firm high-five. "Well done on your full marks!"

Paprika shuffled over to join them. "I'm so glad you're staying with us, Maud."

"Me, too," Maud replied. "Rotwood just wouldn't be the same if I didn't have my best mates with me." Wilf and Paprika smiled.

"I just had an idea," said Wilf. "We're going to Lost Lagoon in Dour Valley for our next holiday. You could both come along if you like."

Paprika's eyes widened. "I don't know ... They say there's a really vicious colony of squirmy swamp things there, with slimy skin and fishy eyes and jagged claws. It's meant to be one of the most frightening holiday destinations in the entire world."

"Really?" asked Maud. "The most frightening of all?"

"That's right," said Paprika.

"In that case," grinned Maud, "you can count me in."

Other titles by A. B. Saddlewick:

ISBN: 978-1-78055-072-5

ISBN: 978-1-78055-073-2

ISBN: 978-1-78055-074-9

ISBN: 978-1-78055-075-6

ISBN: 978-1-78055-173-9